To CLARK,

ENJOY!

Andrea
Toffoli

PRESENTS ®

BENGALMIN FRANKLIN

Based on the life of the great inventor Benjamin Franklin

Written and Illustrated by:
ANDREW TOFFOLI

Graphic Design and Layout by:
J. RODRIGO LIZARRAGA

Color Design:
MARIA JASPER GONZALEZ

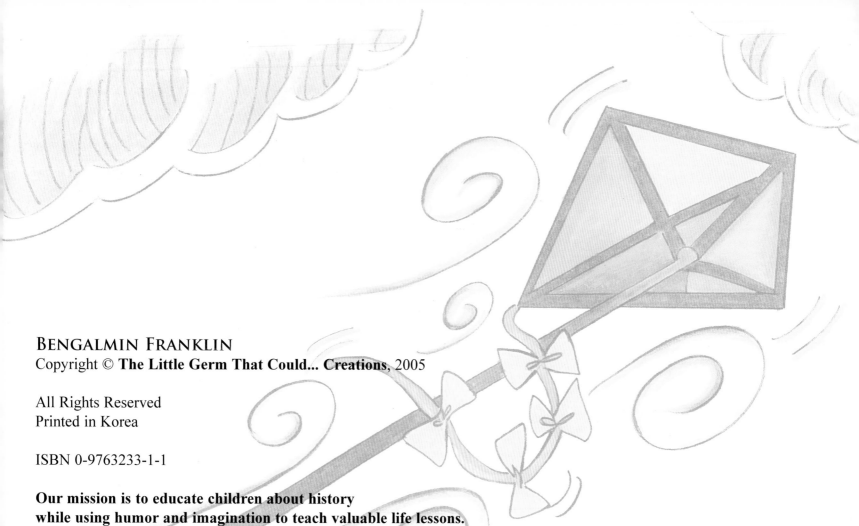

BENGALMIN FRANKLIN

ISBN 0-9763233-1-1

**Our mission is to educate children about history
while using humor and imagination to teach valuable life lessons.**

Please visit us online at **www.littlegerm.com**

10 9 8 7 6 5 4 3 2 1

For Missy

Bengalmin Franklin, a curious feline, was born in Boston, Massachusetts.

As a cub, Bengalmin
loved to read books and
think new ideas.

Bengalmin would read...

...and read

...as many books as he could get his paws on.

THE TAMING OF THE 'ROO

5

All this reading made Ben want to print his own books.

So he moved to Philadelphia to find a job as a printer....
and he did.

While working long hours on the printing press, Ben dreamed of having a print shop where he could create his own books.

So Ben worked and saved...

...and saved and
worked...

...and worked and saved...

...until he had enough money to buy his own print shop.

The first book Ben wrote and printed was called "Poor Richard's Almanac."

Ben Exclaimed, "This almanac is full of weather and information, and will do wonders for your education!"

Ben was very helpful in his community.

He invited everyone to read books for free in his new creation called a library.

He created a hospital where no one had to pay,
even if you had to stay for more than a day.

He opened a school for girls and boys,
and most found it more fun than toys.

And last but not least, to protect man and beast... Ben started Philadelphia's first fire department.

17

Everyone in town would say...
"Your ideas are great and well worth the wait!"

18

And Ben would reply...
"If you think there is no more,
wait 'til you see what I have in store!"

His next invention happened quite by accident while reading...

Ben's vision had become blurry,
and he needed to find a solution in a hurry!

So Ben thought...

...and thought

...and thought

...and thought of a way to see clearer.

There was no solution in sight.

Until one day when Ben was thirsty, he reached for a glass...

Ben excitedly shouted...
"Reading took as long as molasses,
but not now with my new bi-focal glasses!"

"I can now see far and near...

and they fit purrrfectly behind my ear!"

With Ben's new glasses he found it easy to watch the clouds
and lightning for hours and hours.

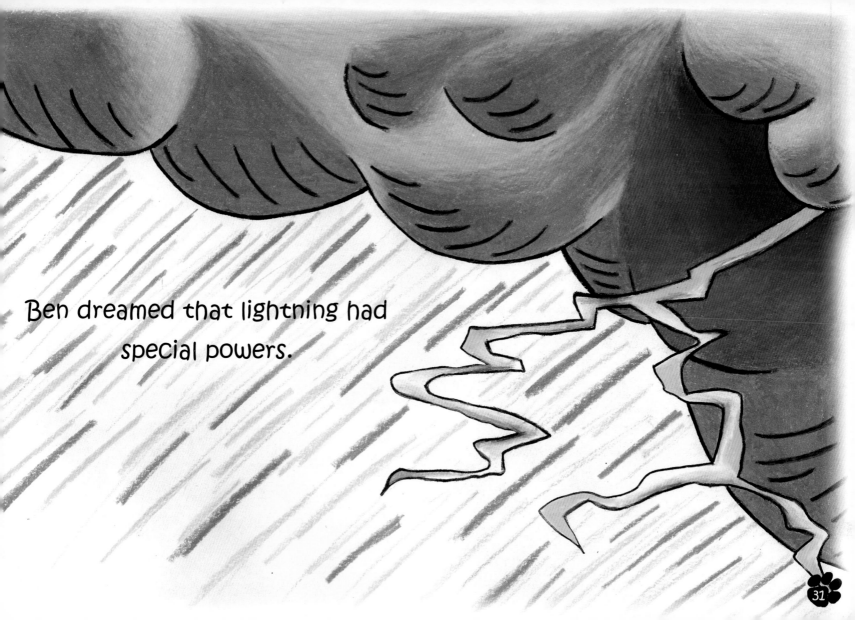

Ben dreamed that lightning had special powers.

A stormy day arrived and Ben
had an experiment in mind.

So he found a perfect spot and raised his kite to the sky, hoping that lightning would pass by.

The wind caught the kite and it flew into the storm!

Lightning struck the kite and sparks flew from the key!

Ben proved that you can move electricity!

While Ben was making discoveries,
nearby in Washington, D.C.
two groups were fighting over the
rules for our country.

37

So Ben arrived and united both sides,
so they could cooperate and create,
the constitution of the United States

Ben declared...
This simple piece of paper will be our country's imagemaker,
and with this creation, we can build a better nation.

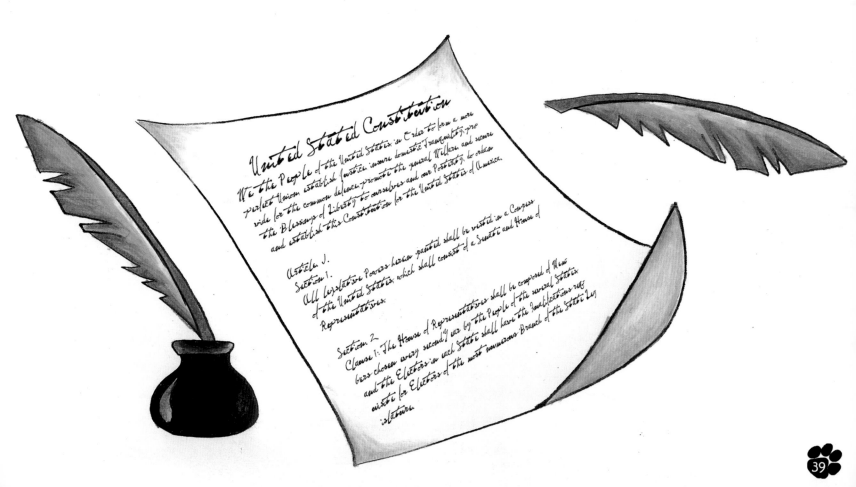

Bengalmin Franklin worked hard to
make his dreams come true,
and invented many great things
for me and you.

COMING SOON!
from
hi·stories
PRESENTS ®

Marco Hippolo ™

George Washing-Ton ™

Tho-mouse Jefferson ™

Lionardo DaVinci ™

Paw-l Revere ™

Bark Twain ™

All artwork and characters are protected under U.S copyright laws. Copyright 2004, The Little Germ That Could... Creations

Juan Ponce De Le-bison™

Alexander Graham Bill™

Lud-pig Van Beethoven™

Jo-horn Sebastian Bach™

George Washington Car-fur™

Thomas Owl-va Edison™

Bee-li Whitney™

Wolfgang Amadeus Mole-zart™

William Shakes-bear™